The Very Windy Day

Library of Congress Cataloging in Publication Data

MacDonald, Elizabeth. The very windy day/by Elizabeth MacDonald;
illustrated by Lesley Summers. p.cm.
Summary: Four people running errands on a very windy day have
their possessions blown away and ultimately returned to them.
ISBN 0-688-11045-2 (lib.).—ISBN 0-688-11044-4 (trade)
[1. Winds—Fiction.]   I. Summers, Lesley, ill.   II. Title.
PZ7.M1465Ve   1992 [E]—dc20 91-690 CIP AC

1 3 5 7 9 10 8 6 4 2

First U.S. Edition, 1992

For Wendy and Debbie
EM

For Mum and Dad
L S

South Street

The Very Windy Day

by ELIZABETH MacDONALD

illustrated by LESLEY SUMMERS

Tambourine Books/New York

It was a very windy morning in Summerville. On the way to buy his weekly ice cream cone, Johnny Brown stopped to get his sister on North Street. "Don't let Emma's ears get cold," his aunt said, and wrapped her up in a blanket.

North Street

When Mrs. Green left the hairdresser on South Street she put on her new hat to keep her hair neat. She was in a hurry to get ready for her niece's party that afternoon. Suddenly a gust of wind swept off the hat and blew it toward East Street.

East Street

On East Street Susan White's new kitten began to meow. As
she lifted the kitten out of its box, the box was whisked away.
So she caught Mrs. Green's hat to protect it from the wind. Then
she continued on her way to buy food for her kitten.

Over on North Street Mr. Black was on his
way to mail a letter. The wind snatched off
the newspaper wrapped around his lunch.
So he grabbed the box to keep his food warm.

North Street

By West Street Emma had squirmed out of her blanket. Johnny thought Mr. Black's newspaper would be just as good to keep his sister warm.

East Street

Mrs. Green had nothing for her head until Emma's blanket sailed by. But when she couldn't grip both her package and the blanket, the wind took the blanket.

Holding her kitten Susan forgot to hang onto the hat. So she caught the blanket for her kitten.

Just as Mr. Black put down the box to mail his letter the wind blew over the box and his lunch tumbled out. But now he had Mrs. Green's hat.

West Street

Johnny's sister kept squirming. The newspaper fell off and flew away. So Johnny seized the kitten's box to put over her ears.

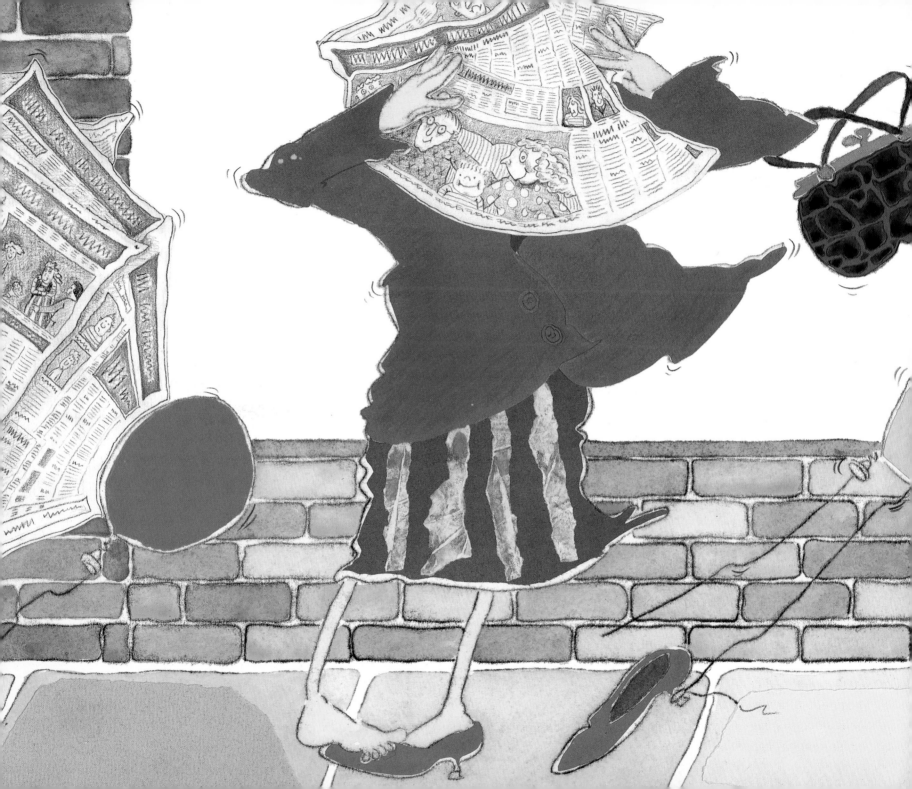

Mrs. Green still had nothing for her hair, so she wrapped the newspaper around her head. But the wind snatched that away too and sent it sailing.

North Street

Susan's kitten was frightened by the wind. When it leapt out of the blanket, it became tangled in Mr. Black's newspaper before the wind carried it down the street.

West Street

Mr. Black's lunch was starting to get cold. When he saw the blanket, he let go of the hat.

The box was not keeping Emma's ears warm. So Johnny grabbed the hat and plopped it on her head.

Mrs. Green's head was still bare. As she put the kitten's box over her head someone bumped into her and knocked it off. Then the box bounced away.

South Street

When Susan reached South Street the kitten's box was lying outside her door. She picked up the box, put in the kitten, and went inside to make its dinner.

On East Street Mr. Black's newspaper had blown against his door. He dropped the blanket, gathered up the paper, and went inside to eat his lunch while he read the news.

East Street

The hat was too big for Emma, so the wind whisked it from her head. But when they got home Johnny found her blanket outside their house, wrapped her up and went in to see his mother.

North Street

Suddenly the wind stopped. Mrs. Green found her hat and went into her house. "What a perfect afternoon for a party," she said.